PANDA FEELS JEALOUS

A book about JEALOUSY

Written by Sue Graves

Illustrated by Trevor Dunton

W

FRANKLIN WATTS

LONDON•SYDNEY

Panda was jealous of **everyone**! She was jealous of her baby brother. She said Mum spent **more time** with him than with her!

Mum said babies needed lots of help when they were little. But Panda was cross. She **stamped her feet**. She said it **wasn't fair**.

Panda was jealous of her big sister.
Her big sister could **stay up later**
than her.

Panda said it wasn't fair. She said she
wanted to stay up late, too. Mum said she
could stay up later **when she was older**.

At school, Bear had a sparkly pencil. She said her granny had given it to her. But Panda was jealous. She wanted a sparkly pencil like Bear's. She said Bear's pencil was **horrid**. Bear was **upset**.

9

Panda liked playing basketball. She was good at **passing** the ball. But she was jealous of Gecko.

He was good at **scoring** goals. Everyone said he was the best goalscorer ever!

Panda wanted to be the best goalscorer.

She said Gecko wasn't good at basketball.

Gecko was upset.

Everyone was cross with Panda.

They said it **wasn't nice** to be jealous of others.

They said she **couldn't play** if she was going
to be unkind.

Panda was **upset**. She didn't like everyone being cross with her. She didn't like **feeling jealous** either. It made her tummy ache, and she felt horrid inside. She went to see Miss Bird.

Panda told Miss Bird about feeling jealous.
Miss Bird **listened carefully**.
She said everyone felt jealous sometimes.

But she said it was much better to be pleased with all the things you **did have**, and all the things you **could do**, rather than be jealous of others. She said it was nice to be **pleased for others**, too!

Panda thought about all the lovely things
she had. She thought about her baby brother.
She **was glad** she had a baby brother really.
He was good fun.

18

She thought about her big sister, too. She knew it **was fair** that her big sister could stay up longer.

Then she thought about Bear and Gecko. She felt sad. She wished she hadn't been unkind.

Then Miss Bird asked Panda what she should do to **put things right**. Panda had a think. She said she should **say sorry** to everyone for being jealous and unkind. Miss Bird said those were good ideas.

She said she should **remember** to think about all the things she did have and all the things she could do. She said she would try to be **pleased for others**, too.

21

The next day, Panda **helped Mum** with her baby brother. She helped to feed him.

She helped to dress him.

Mum said she was a **good sister**.

Panda felt proud. She didn't feel jealous at all.

At school, Turtle showed Panda her new hat.
She was very pleased with it.

Panda didn't feel jealous. She was **pleased** for Turtle. She said Turtle's hat was **beautiful**. Turtle smiled. She said Panda was very kind.

That afternoon, everyone played basketball. Panda was **pleased** that she could pass the ball well. She passed the ball to Gecko again and again. Gecko scored lots of goals.

Everyone **clapped** and **cheered**. Panda was pleased for Gecko. She said it was a **much nicer feeling** to be pleased for others than to be jealous.

A note about sharing this book

The *Behaviour Matters* series has been developed to provide a starting point for further discussion on children's behaviour both in relation to themselves and others. The series is set in the jungle with animal characters reflecting typical behaviour traits often seen in young children.

Panda Feels Jealous

This story looks at some of the reasons many children feel jealous and looks at ways they can overcome this emotion.

How to use the book

The book is designed for adults to share with either an individual child, or a group of children, and as a starting point for discussion.

The book also provides visual support and repeated words and phrases to build reading confidence.

Before reading the story

Choose a time to read when you and the children are relaxed and have time to share the story.

Spend time looking at the illustrations and talk about what the book might be about before reading it together.

Encourage children to employ a phonics first approach to tackling new words by sounding the words out.

After reading, talk about the book with the children:

- Talk about the story with the children. What is the book about?

- Talk about the things that make Panda feel jealous. How many of the children have felt jealous about the same things? Encourage them to share their feelings with the others and to try and explain why they felt jealous.

- Talk about the way Panda dealt with her jealousy initially. Do the children think she was unkind? Why / why not?

- Together look at how Panda dealt with her jealousy after talking to Miss Bird. Why were these good ideas? Why is it good to feel pleased for others?

- How do the children overcome any jealous feelings they might have? Encourage them to share their ideas with the others.

- Ask the children to draw a picture of something or someone they have felt jealous about. Next, ask them to draw a picture to show how they overcame their jealousy. Examples might be the arrival of a new baby in the house in the first picture followed by the child helping Mum or Dad with the baby in the second.

- Invite children to show their pictures to the others and to explain their drawings.

For Isabelle, William A, William G, George, Max, Emily,

Leo, Caspar, Felix, Tabitha, Phoebe and Harry –S.G.

Franklin Watts
First published in 2022 by
The Watts Publishing Group

Text © Franklin Watts 2022
Illustrations © Trevor Dunton 2022

The right of Trevor Dunton to be identified as the illustrator
of this Work has been asserted in accordance with the
Copyright, Designs and Patents Act, 1988.

Editor: Jackie Hamley
Designer: Cathryn Gilbert and Peter Scoulding

A CIP catalogue record for this book is available
from the British Library.

ISBN 978 1 4451 7967 4 (hardback)
ISBN 978 1 4451 7968 1 (paperback)
ISBN 978 1 4451 8375 6 (ebook)

Printed in China

Franklin Watts is a division of
Hachette Children's Books,
an Hachette UK company.
www.hachette.co.uk